Jez Alborough

DUCK'S D,

Collins

An imprint of HarperCollinsPublishers

Say hello to Mr Duck.

Where's he going in his truck?

On a boat trip. Beep, beep, beep.

Look who's going too, it's Sheep.

'Hooray!' calls Duck 'we're getting near. I can see the sea from here.

Let's start the boat. Let's go,' he said.

He didn't see the rock ahead.

The boat went BANG.

Duck went QUACK.

Sheep felt ill.

So Duck turned back.

Quack, quack, nibble, poor old Sheep.

Time to go. Brrrm, brrrm, beep, beep.

WATCH OUT here comes DUCK!

Hardback: 0-00-198346-6 £10.99; Paperback: 0-00-664717-0 £4.99

This is the tale of a duck in a truck –
a truck that was stuck in some yucky brown muck.

A leaking roof? A window stuck?
These are jobs for Fix-It Duck!

Hardback: 0-00-710623-8 £9.99; Paperback: 0-00-710624-6 £4.99

Kate Greenaway Medal – Highly Commended

Who knows what dangers are afloat
when Duck is Captain of the boat?

Hardback: 0-00-713010-4 £9.99; Paperback: 0-00-713011-2 £4.99

'Alborough's pictures are addictive... *Duck in the Truck* is a
picture book where rhyme, illustration, wit and inventiveness
combine to produce outstanding quality.' *TES Primary*